My Furry Foster Family

Murray the Ferret

by Debbi Michiko Florence

illustrated by Melanie Demmer

raintree

a Capstone company — publishers for children

For ferret knowledge, to former zoo colleague and forever friend, Diane Kisich Davis — DMF

Raintree is an imprint of Capstone Global Library Limited, a company incorporated in England and Wales having its registered office at 264 Banbury Road, Oxford, OX2 7DY — Registered company number: 6695582

www.raintree.co.uk
myorders@raintree.co.uk

Text © Capstone Global Library Limited 2021
The moral rights of the proprietor have been asserted.

All rights reserved. No part of this publication may be reproduced in any form or by any means (including photocopying or storing it in any medium by electronic means and whether or not transiently or incidentally to some other use of this publication) without the written permission of the copyright owner, except in accordance with the provisions of the Copyright, Designs and Patents Act 1988 or under the terms of a licence issued by the Copyright Licensing Agency, 5th Floor, Shackleton House, 4 Battle Bridge Lane, London SE1 2HX (www.cla.co.uk). Applications for the copyright owner's written permission should be addressed to the publisher.

Edited by Jill Kalz
Designed by Lori Bye
Original illustrations © Capstone Global Library Limited 2021
Production by Tori Abraham
Originated by Capstone Global Library Ltd

Image credits
Melanie Demmer, 71; Roy Thomas, 70

978 1 3982 0461 4

British Library Cataloguing in Publication Data
A full catalogue record for this book is available from the British Library.

Printed in the United Kingdom

Contents

Dad
(Tim Takano)

Mum
(Cindy Takano)

Me
(Kaita Takano)

Eraser

Ollie

Joss Lawrence,
Happy Tails
Rescue

Hannah Miller,
my best friend

CHAPTER 1

Hello, Murray!

I finished the last cheese cracker on my plate. Delicious!

Ollie, my mini dachshund, licked cracker crumbs from the floor. He's a good dog. He always likes to help clean up.

I wiped my hands on a napkin and turned to my mum. "I'm ready for my books," I said.

"You've finished your snack already?" Mum said. "That was quick, Kaita." She handed me two books. They were about ferrets.

I flipped through the first one. I had already read both books a few times. My mum works at a bookshop. Whenever we get a new foster pet, Mum brings home books for me to read. I learn a lot from them. I learn even more when the animals come to our house.

Mum, Dad and I are a foster family for pets. That means we take care of homeless animals until they find their forever family.

"Do you think we're ready for a ferret?" Mum asked me.

"Yes!" I said. "I've read these books so many times. All the ferret facts are up here in my head."

Yip! Yip! Yip! Ollie ran to the front door. Ollie always lets us know when someone comes to our house. He has good hearing. He barks even before the person rings the doorbell.

"That must be Joss with our new foster pet!" Mum said.

Mum and I went to the door. Ollie wagged his tail. He remembered Joss. She once fostered him. That is how we adopted Ollie from Happy Tails Rescue. After we met Joss, we wanted to be a foster family too.

"Hello, Mrs Takano, Kaita and Ollie," Joss said. She held a big, tall cage. Mum helped Joss carry it into the spare room. We usually keep our foster pets in there.

I hurried after them. I wanted to see the ferret!

Yip! Yip! Yip! Ollie wanted to see the new foster pet too. But he knew he had to wait. Whenever we get a new pet, Ollie has to wait until the animal gets settled. Ollie is clever. He went to my room to play with his favourite tennis ball.

"Good boy, Ollie," I said. I walked into the spare room and closed the door behind me.

A cute little ferret sat in the far corner of the cage. He was mostly browny-black, with a lighter band of fur around his belly. He looked like he was wearing an eye mask.

"Kaita, meet Murray the ferret," Joss said. "He's still pretty young. The vet thinks he's about one year old."

Murray walked over to me and stood on his hind legs.

"Hello, Murray," I said. "My name is Kaita. I'm glad you're here."

"This is your first time with a ferret, right?" Joss asked.

"Yes," Mum said. "But we've all been reading books about how to look after one. Kaita, especially, has read a lot over the past few days."

"Where did Murray come from?" I asked. "What happened to his owner?"

"We don't know about Murray's first owner," Joss said. "A woman called Annie brought him to us. She found him in her garden. She lives near a park."

"How did he get there?" I asked.

"Well, we think he either escaped from his home or someone let him go," Joss said. "We tried to find his owner but had no luck."

"Why would someone let him go?" I asked. I thought of Murray, wandering outside alone. I thought about how scared he must've been. My stomach started to hurt. "Why would someone do that, just leave him in the wild? Oh, poor Murray."

Joss nodded sadly. "I know. It's horrible," she said. "Sometimes owners let their pets go. They don't understand that these animals can't live in the wild. They are pets. They are used to being looked after."

Joss put her arm around my shoulder. "He's lucky he found Annie," she continued. "Or rather, it's lucky that Annie found him! Sadly, she couldn't give him a forever home. It was good that she brought him to us."

"And now we will take care of Murray until he finds his forever home!" I said. "This is going to be great!"

CHAPTER 2

A pocket-sized pet

I couldn't wait one more minute to hold Murray. I turned to Joss. "Can we let him out of his cage now?" I asked.

Murray pawed at the side of the cage. It was like he understood what I had asked! His nose wiggled.

"Yes, Kaita," Joss said. "You can let him out any time."

"Cool!" I said, bouncing up and down.

"Just make sure there are no electrical cords for him to chew," Joss said. "Also, you need to watch him closely when he's out."

"Why?" I asked.

Joss grinned. "Annie learned the hard way," she said. "Murray chewed his way into her sofa. Then he made a nest inside it."

Mum picked up the pillows from the sofa bed. "I guess we'd better put these away," she said.

Joss laughed and nodded. She opened the cage and took Murray out. He looked like a long Slinky toy.

"He's the same shape as Ollie," I said. "Long and narrow."

"That's true," Joss said. She held up Murray, his body hanging from her hands. "But Murray is more flexible. Being able to bend easily lets him get into tight spaces."

I sat on the floor, and Joss showed me how to hold Murray. I held his body with one arm and put my other hand on top. He snuggled against me.

"He's so sweet," I said.

Then, quick as a flash, Murray wriggled and popped out of my arms. Good thing I was sitting down! He skipped and jumped around the room, sideways and forwards.

"Do you spot anything extra special about Murray?" Joss asked. "Have a good look."

I watched Murray as he ran around the room. He climbed over a basket of magazines. He sniffed the wastebasket. He ran around Mum's feet. He was fast!

"Oh," Mum said. She leaned down to look closer at Murray. "Is he missing a foot?"

I scooped Murray up. Mum was right. Our little ferret was missing his back left foot.

"Is he OK?" I asked. I didn't want him to be in pain. "How did that happen?"

"The vet checked and said Murray is fine," Joss said. "We don't know how he lost his foot. It's a mystery."

Mum went with Joss to get the rest of Murray's things from Joss' truck. I sat on the floor with Murray. I wanted to watch him run around some more.

Murray had a different idea, though. He climbed into my lap. Then he pushed his nose into the front pocket of my hoodie.

"Hey, Murray, what are you doing?" I asked him.

Murray kept pushing his way into the pocket. Before long, he had slid all the way in and disappeared.

I peeked inside.

Murray was curled up, with his eyes closed. He'd fallen asleep!

I cradled my pocket and walked into the living room. Mum was saying goodbye to Joss.

"Look," I said in a loud whisper. I pointed at my front pocket.

Joss smiled. "Sweet," she said quietly. "Ferrets can be very playful, but then they get sleepy and nap. I think he's going to have fun with you, Kaita. Thank you for looking after him."

"I'll do my best," I said.

After Joss left, I did my homework at the kitchen table. Murray seemed warm and happy inside my hoodie, so I let him sleep.

Ollie came into the kitchen, looking for a treat. He walked over to my chair and nudged my leg with his nose. He wagged his tail fast. That's when Murray wriggled and poked his head out of my hoodie pocket.

Ollie looked a little surprised.

"Be gentle, Ollie," I said. Joss had told us that Murray was OK with friendly dogs. Ollie was very friendly. We weren't worried about the two animals not getting on.

Murray crawled out of my pocket and onto my lap.

Ollie backed off. He still wagged his tail but not quite as fast as before.

Then Murray slipped onto the floor. He skipped sideways at Ollie.

Ollie didn't know what to do. He backed off some more. His tail wagged very slowly.

I giggled.

"Ollie, it's OK," I said. "I think Murray wants to play with you."

As soon as I said that, Murray started running round the kitchen table. Ollie watched for a second. Then he started running round the table too, chasing Murray!

Round and round they went. Sometimes, Murray would hop at Ollie and Ollie would skid to a stop. Then they'd run the other way.

All I could do was laugh. They were so funny! Murray and my little dog were becoming friends fast.

After a while, Murray got tired. He crawled up my leg and back into my hoodie pocket.

"Kaita, it's time for dinner," Mum said. "Put Murray back in his cage for a bit, please."

I took Murray to the spare room and put him back in his cage. He curled up in his bed straight away.

"Sleep well, Murray," I said.

I had a feeling he and I were going to have a lot of fun together.

CHAPTER 3

Fostering fun

Murray *was* a lot of fun. He loved to run around the house. He loved climbing on things. He also loved to eat hard-boiled eggs. That was one of the snacks he could have. When it was time to put him back in his cage, I simply held out an egg treat. He always came running to me.

In my room, I made an obstacle course for Murray. I got some old cardboard boxes and cut out different-sized holes in them. I lined them up.

"OK, Murray," I said. I put him down on my bedroom floor. "What do you think of this?"

Murray sniffed the first box. He walked around and sniffed the other boxes too.

He poked his head through one of the box holes. Then he climbed inside. After a few seconds, he popped out of a hole on the other side of the box. He did the same thing in the next box and the next. Murray seemed to love the boxes!

I ran to the kitchen. Dad was making coffee. "Dad! Come and see Murray!" I said.

Dad followed me to my room. We sat down on the floor by the boxes.

"He loves these boxes," I said.

We waited for Murray to pop his head out of one of them. It was quiet.

"Where is he?" Dad asked.

I slid over and looked in every box. But there was no Murray. "Oh no!" I cried. "He's not here!"

"I'm sure he's around," Dad said calmly. "Let's go and check the spare room."

I sprang off the floor and ran to the spare room. I was so worried. What would Joss do if I lost a foster pet?

When I got to the doorway, my worries disappeared. Murray was in his cage. He was eating his food.

"Oh, he must have got hungry," I said.

Dad closed the cage. "I'm glad he's safe," he said.

I was glad too. It was a good reminder that ferrets are fast. I had to keep a closer watch on Murray when he was out of his cage.

Later that night, I couldn't find my pyjama top. "I left it right here on my bed," I told Mum.

"Did you put it in the laundry basket?" Mum asked.

"Maybe," I said. But I didn't remember doing that. I got a clean pyjama top from my cupboard and put it on. I climbed into bed with Ollie and read my book.

*

The next morning, Dad took Ollie for a walk. I had an idea.

"Mum!" I said. "We can teach Murray how to walk on a lead. That way, he won't get away from me in the house. Maybe we can take him outside too."

"That's a great idea," Mum said. "We have an old harness that is much too small for Ollie. Let's try it on Murray and see if it fits."

We walked into the spare room.
Murray was climbing around inside
his cage. I was glad he was awake.
I got him out, and Mum helped me
put the harness on Murray.

It fit!

Next, Mum clipped an old lead onto the harness. We put Murray on the floor. He twisted and turned. He tried to bite the lead.

"Hey, Murray," I said in a soft voice. "It's not so bad. Let's go for a walk. Follow me."

I walked a little and gently tugged on the lead. Murray stopped trying to bite it. He looked at me.

"Come on," I said.

Murray made a sound like he was laughing and started to follow me. It was the first time I heard him make a sound. It was so cute!

He got used to the lead quickly. We walked all over the house. It was fun taking a ferret for a walk!

After a few days, Murray got used to life with my family. Every afternoon, he slept inside my hoodie pocket while I did my homework. I wore that hoodie after school every day, just for Murray. After supper, I walked him. And he and Ollie played.

At bedtime, I let Murray run around his room for a while. I gave him a bit of hard-boiled egg. Then I put him back in his cage.

"Goodnight, Murray," I said. "See you in the morning!"

CHAPTER 4

What's that smell?

One day, I decided to draw a
picture of Murray. I love to draw.
I always draw pictures of our foster
pets. It's a way to remember them
after they've found their forever
homes. I went into the spare room.
I kept my special sketchbook next to
the sofa bed.

Murray was napping. Perfect! A sleeping Murray would make a cute picture.

I sat down on the sofa bed and opened my sketchbook. I reached for my favourite pencil. It wasn't there. I looked to see if it had fallen on the floor. I didn't see it.

Murray woke up. He walked to the cage door and looked at me.

I laughed. "You're right, Murray," I said. "I can draw later. Time for snuggles!"

I scooped him up and lifted him to my face. Our noses touched.

"Ew!" I said, turning my head. "You kind of stink!"

Murray blinked at me. I think I hurt his feelings.

"Sorry," I said. "You do kind of smell bad, though."

I hugged Murray to me, but not close to my face. I grabbed his harness. Where was his lead? It wasn't next to his harness, where I had left it. "I seem to be losing a lot of things lately!" I said.

I carried Murray to the living room. Dad was doing a puzzle. Mum was at work. Sometimes she takes Ollie with her. That's where he was that day.

"Dad?" I said. "I think something is wrong with Murray. He smells funny."

I got a shallow plastic box and put it in the bath. Dad filled the box with lukewarm water. I got a small toy boat and put it in the water. Then we put Murray into the bath. We weren't sure how he would feel about a bath. Some ferrets don't like water.

Murray sniffed every part of the bath. When he got to the plastic box, he slapped the toy boat with his paw. The boat bobbed. Murray rounded his back and slapped the boat again.

"OK, Murray," I said, giggling. "Bath time."

I picked Murray up and gently placed him in the water.

Straight away, Murray started

paddling around. He rolled over and splashed. Someone was having a great time!

Dad handed me the special shampoo that Joss had brought. He held Murray, while I rubbed shampoo all over Murray's fur. I was careful not to get it in his eyes or ears.

Once Murray was all soapy, Dad put him back in the water. Murray splashed around. I rinsed him off.

Bathing a ferret wasn't as hard as bathing a dog, at least. We once had a foster dog who did not want to have a bath! That was a big job!

I got a fluffy towel and wrapped

Murray in it. He wriggled around inside.

"I think he wants to be on the ground," Dad said. "Put the towel down too."

I did. Murray rolled around on the towel. He looked funny with his damp fur sticking up. He burrowed under the towel. After a couple seconds, he poked his head out once, then twice. The third time, he grabbed a corner of the towel and dragged it out of the bathroom.

"Hey," I said, laughing. "Come back here, you thief!"

CHAPTER 5

Mystery solved

Murray ran into the spare room. He dashed under the sofa bed with the bath towel.

"Silly Murray," I said. "I need that towel back."

I got down on the floor and peeked under the sofa bed at Murray. There he was with the towel – and a lot of other things!

"What have you got under there, Murray?" I asked.

I reached in and started pulling things out, one by one.

My pyjama top.

My favourite drawing pencil.

Murray's lead.

Ollie's squeaky hot dog toy.

One of Mum's socks.

These were all the things that I had lost – and more!

Murray slid out and crawled into my lap. I laughed.

"I have solved the mystery of the missing things," I said. "You are the thief! I should've known it was you, you sneaky boy."

I cuddled my cleaned-up foster ferret, then put him back in his cage. I went to tell Dad my news.

"That's right," Dad said. "We read that too. Ferrets like to take things and hide them. Mum was looking everywhere for her sock last night."

"What about my sock?" Mum asked, walking into the room. She was back from work with Ollie.

Dad and I told her about Murray's stash under the sofa.

"I'm glad you solved that mystery," Mum said. "And that reminds me, the Mystery Book Club meets at the bookshop tonight. Should we take Murray to meet them? They always love to hear about a good mystery."

I nodded. "That's a good idea, Mum," I said. "We've had Murray for a few weeks now. Not a lot of people are looking for a pet ferret."

"Well, I'll let you tell the story to the club tonight, OK?" Mum said.

"OK!" I said.

*

That evening at the bookshop, I put Murray and his carrier behind the counter. I wanted to keep him a secret for a while.

Ten people from the book club arrived. All of them loved books. They especially loved reading and talking about mysteries. I hoped at least one of them would want a pet ferret.

I giggled. "No," I said.

"That was a good guess, Maria," a man said. "Everyone was missing something, except for the dad."

"Can you give us a clue?" a teenage girl asked.

"I will give you a big clue," I said. I went behind the counter and brought out the carrier. I held it up so everyone could see Murray.

"We are a foster family," I continued. "We take care of pets until they find their forever homes. Murray is a ferret. We hope he finds a home, but we are also having a lot of fun with him."

Maria, the woman with the purple hat, cried, "Murray is the thief!"

The man turned in his chair. "How do you know, Maria?" he asked. "Maybe Kaita is trying to trick us."

Maria smiled wider. "I know because I used to have a ferret," she said. "Ferrets love, love, love to steal things."

"Maria, you had a ferret?" Mum asked. "I didn't know that!"

Maria nodded. "It was a long time ago," she said. "He was the best pet I ever had."

"Would you like to meet Murray?" I asked.

"I would love that," Maria said.

I opened Murray's carrier, reached in and carefully lifted him out. Then I put him in Maria's lap.

Guess what? He curled up and fell asleep on her!

For the rest of the meeting, Murray napped on Maria. She kept stroking him and smiling at him. My heart filled with hope.

*

The next day, Maria came to our house. This time she wore an orange hat with a feather in it.

"I couldn't stop thinking about Murray," Maria said. "He was so sweet last night, sleeping in my lap."

"Joss already said you could take him home, if you like," Mum said. "She thinks you two would be an excellent match."

"Oh, I would like that very much," Maria said.

I handed Murray to Maria. He climbed up on her shoulder and tucked himself under her hair. He seemed very happy. And that made *me* very happy.

Saying goodbye to Murray was tough. But I was glad he had a new home. And I was extra-glad he had a new home with someone who understood ferrets.

Maybe one day my family will get another ferret to foster. I never know what kind of pet will come and stay with us next!

Think about it!

1. In what ways does Murray look like and act like a thief?
2. Why does Kaita's mum think taking Murray to the Mystery Book Club meeting is a good idea?
3. Would you want a pet ferret? Why or why not?

Draw it! Write it!

1. Murray is a bit of a thief. Draw a picture of Murray with something he might steal from your house.
2. Write a short letter to Maria. Tell her all the things you think she should know about Murray.

Glossary

adopt   take and raise as one's own

carrier   box or bag that carries or holds something

dachshund   type of dog with a long body and short legs

flexible   able to bend easily

foster   give care and a safe home for a short time

futon   thin, cotton-filled mattress used on the floor or in a wooden frame for sleeping

harness   set of straps wrapped around a pet's body and attached to a lead

obstacle course   set of things that someone must jump over, climb or crawl through

territory   area of land that an animal claims as its own to live in

vet   person trained to take care of the health of animals

A closer look at ferrets

Ferrets are members of the weasel family. They have long, narrow bodies. They are quick and flexible. They can also be a little smelly. Weasels in the wild mark their territory with strong scent glands. The smells tell other weasels to keep out of the area.

Eraser

Ferrets can make good pets, but they need
special care. They love to chew and burrow
and can get into hard-to-reach places. It's
important that pet ferrets have time to
run around. It is also important to keep
an eye on them. They can get into trouble.
They might chew or steal things or get
stuck in sofas or other narrow spaces.

Pet ferrets are curious and friendly.
They can sleep on their owner's lap
for long periods of time. They can be
litter box-trained and learn to walk
on a lead. They can also learn tricks.

Kaita's favourites

Kaita Takano is a made-up
character. She is based on
a real-life Kaita, who also
fosters pets with her family.

Author Debbi Michiko Florence
asked Real Kaita what some
of her favourite things are.
Then Debbi imagined how
Murray the ferret would
answer the same questions.

What would *your* answers be?

What is your favourite food?

Kaita - sushi (and anything else
with white rice)

Murray - boiled eggs

What is your favourite book?

Kaita - anything with monsters or scary clowns

Murray - any book I can get my teeth into (and chew)

What is your favourite game?

Kaita - *Minecraft*

Murray - taking things that belong to the Takano family and hiding them under the sofa bed

What is your favourite thing to do outdoors?

Kaita - gardening

Murray - digging in the garden

What is your favourite thing to do indoors?

Kaita - knitting, crocheting or watching YouTube videos

Murray - sleeping in Kaita's hoodie pocket

About the author

Debbi Michiko Florence writes books for children in her writing studio, The Word Nest. She is an animal lover with a degree in zoology and has worked at a pet shop, the Humane Society, a raptor rehabilitation centre and a zoo. She is the author of two chapter book series: Jasmine Toguchi and Dorothy & Toto. Debbi lives in Connecticut, USA, with her husband, a rescue dog, a rabbit and two ducks.

About the illustrator

Melanie Demmer is an illustrator and designer
living in Los Angeles, USA. She graduated with a
BFA in illustration from the College for Creative
Studies in Detroit and has been creating artwork for
various clothing, animation and publishing projects
ever since. When she isn't making art, Melanie
enjoys writing, spending time in the great outdoors,
iced tea, scary films and having naps with her
cat, Pepper.

Go on all the fun, furry foster adventures!

Apple and Annie, the Hamster Duo

Betty the Bearded Dragon

Buttons the Kitten

Kingston the Great Dane

Murray the Ferret

Roo the Rabbit

Tiki the Cockatoo

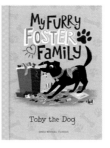

Toby the Dog

Only from Raintree!